PEANUTS®

You Got a Rock, CHARLIE BROWN!

by Charles M. Schulz

adapted by Maggie Testa

illustrated by Robert Pope

Ready-to-Read

Simon Spotlight

New York London Toronto Sydney New Delhi

SIMON SPOTLIGHT
An imprint of Simon & Schuster Children's Publishing Division
1230 Avenue of the Americas, New York, New York 10020
This Simon Spotlight edition July 2015
© 2015 Peanuts Worldwide LLC
This is an adaption of the animated special "It's the Great Pumpkin, Charlie Brown"
SIMON SPOTLIGHT, READY-TO-READ, and colophon are registered trademarks of Simon & Schuster, Inc.
For information about special discounts for bulk purchases, please contact Simon & Schuster Special Sales at
1-866-506-1949 or business@simonandschuster.com.
Manufactured in the United States of America 0615 LAK
2 4 6 8 10 9 7 5 3 1
ISBN 978-1-4814-3603-8 (hc)
ISBN 978-1-4814-3602-1 (pbk)
ISBN 978-1-4814-3604-5 (eBook)

The leaves are changing colors
and falling from the trees.
There's a chill in the air.
There are pumpkins all around.
It's Halloween!
Charlie Brown loves Halloween.

Tonight, Charlie Brown is going trick-or-treating.

First he needs to figure out
what to wear.

Charlie Brown decides to dress up
as a ghost.
It should be an easy costume
to make.
All he needs to do is cut two
eyeholes out of a sheet.

Charlie Brown meets up
with his friends.
"Really, Charlie Brown, what are
you supposed to be?" asks Lucy.
"A ghost," Charlie Brown replies.
"I guess I had a little trouble
with the scissors."

Lucy is dressed up as a witch.

"A person should always pick
a costume which is in direct contrast
to one's own personality," she says.

Someone else dressed up
as a ghost joins the group.
"Hi, Pigpen," says Frieda.

"How did you know it was me?"
Pigpen asks.
Even a sheet can't cover the
cloud of dirt that always
surrounds Pigpen!

Snoopy is also in the
Halloween spirit.
He wears a red scarf, goggles,
and a green cap.

"It's the World War One Flying Ace,"
explains Charlie Brown.
"Now I've heard everything!"
says Lucy.

Time for trick-or-treating!
The group of friends walks
to the first house.
Lucy rings the doorbell.

"Trick or treat," everyone shouts
when the door opens.
Everyone gets a little something
in his or her bag.

On the way to the next house,
everyone compares their treats.
"I got five pieces of candy,"
says Lucy.

"I got a chocolate bar,"
says Violet.
"I got a quarter,"
says Pigpen.

Charlie Brown looks in his bag.
He can't believe his eyes.
"I got a rock," he moans.

The group goes to the next house.
"Trick or treat," everyone shouts
when the door opens.
Once again, everyone gets a little
something in his or her bag.

"I got a candy bar,"
says Lucy.

"I got three cookies,"
says Violet.

"I got a pack of gum,"
says Pigpen.

Charlie Brown looks in his bag.
"I got a rock," says Charlie Brown.
"Not again!"

Charlie Brown hopes things will be different at the next house. "Trick or treat," everyone shouts when the door opens.

"I got a popcorn ball," says Lucy.
"I got a fudge bar," says Violet.

Charlie Brown looks in his bag.
This time, he is not surprised.
"I got a rock," he tells everyone.

After trick-or-treating,
Charlie Brown and his bag of rocks
goes to Violet's Halloween party.
Lucy asks if Charlie Brown wants to
be a model.

Charlie Brown is honored,
but not for long.
Lucy only wants to draw
a face on the back of his head.
"Thank you, Charlie Brown,"
says Lucy.
"You made an excellent model."

The next day, Charlie Brown tells
Linus all about the night before.

"Another Halloween has come and gone and all I got was a bag full of rocks," he says.

At least there's always next year!